SOFIA MARTINEZ

My Fantá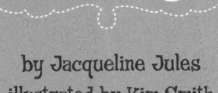stica Family

by Jacqueline Jules

illustrated by Kim Smith

PICTURE WINDOW BOOKS
a capstone imprint

Sofia Martinez is published by
Picture Window Books, a Capstone Imprint
1710 Roe Crest Drive
North Mankato, MN 56003
www.capstoneyoungreaders.com

Library of Congress Cataloging-in-
Publication data is available on the
Library of Congress website

ISBN 978-1-5158-0746-9 (paperback)

Summary: Sofia Martinez loves her familia!
Her cousins, aunts, uncles, and abuela are
a huge part of her life. Whether they are
at a sunny beach or stuck in a dark house
without electricity, the Martinez family
knows how to make the best of every
situation.

Designer: Kay Fraser

Printed and bound in China.
009968S17

TABLE OF CONTENTS

The Beach Trip

CHAPTER 1

Packing Problems

The yearly beach trip was
tomorrow. It took six hours to get
to the beach house, but the trip was
worth it. Sixteen family members
in one house was so fun!

Sofia carried a pile of board games upstairs.

"You're supposed to be packing for the beach," **Mamá** said.

"**Yo sé**," Sofia said. "I need these for the trip."

Mamá frowned. "You need clothes and a swimsuit. Not games."

"But the twins will be there! Camila and Valeria love games," Sofia said.

"That's when it is cold. You should be outside when it's warm," **Mamá** said.

"**Por favor**," Sofia begged.

"You can bring one game," **Mamá** said.

But it wasn't easy to choose. Camila liked one game better. Valeria liked another one. And Sofia couldn't leave behind her own favorite game.

"I'll need all three," she said.

Sofia put them into her suitcase.

She had no room left for clothes.

"Can I put some shorts and shirts in your suitcase?" Sofia asked her big sister, Luisa.

"I have room for one outfit,"
Luisa said.

Her other sister, Elena, packed
Sofia's swimsuit. Now Sofia was
packed and ready to go!

Sofia would not have many clothes for her trip. But she would have plenty of games, and that is what she really needed.

CHAPTER 2

Too Much Stuff

The next morning, **Papá** and

Tío Miguel were packing the cars

in the driveway. They packed

suitcases, beach bags, and coolers.

The trunks were stuffed!

"¡No más!" Papá said.

"But we haven't put in Mariela's stroller or our beach bags," Tía Carmen said.

"I think we need to drive three cars," **Mamá** said.

"¡Claro!" **Tío** Miguel agreed. "We can follow each other."

He went across the yard to get his car.

"I'll take baby Mariela and Manuel," **Tía** Carmen said. "Who else wants to go with me?"

Sofia shook her head. Manuel got car sick, and Baby Mariela cried a lot.

"I'd love to," **Mamá** said.

That left Sofia's two oldest
cousins, her two big sisters, **Tío**
Miguel, **Papá**, and **Abuela**.

"The girls can ride with me," Papá said. "The boys can go with Tío Miguel and Abuela."

They were finally ready to go! Before long, Sofia was sorry she was riding with her sisters.

"Luisa is bothering me," Elena said.

"Elena is bothering me more!" Luisa said.

They were so loud, Sofia couldn't read her book.

At the first stop, Sofia hopped into Tío Miguel's car.

"Do you have room for one more?" Sofia asked.

"¡Claro!" Tío Miguel said.

But the ride wasn't much better.

Hector and Alonzo squirmed and

kicked each other.

After lunch, Sofia asked to ride in the last car. Baby Mariela and Manuel fell asleep.

"Finally!" Sofia said, smiling. "Silencio."

CHAPTER 3

No Sun

They arrived at the beach house before dinner. The twins and their parents were already there.

"After that long drive, nobody is up for cooking. Let's go out for dinner," **Abuela** said.

The twins changed into sundresses. Sofia only had one outfit for the whole week, so she couldn't change.

"I brought an extra dress," Camila said. "You can borrow it."

"**Gracias**," Sofia said.

At dinner, the family talked
about going to the beach the
next day. They couldn't wait for the
soft sand, big waves, and hot sun.

When they went to bed, Sofia realized she was missing something else.

"Do you have extra pajamas?" she asked Valeria.

"I sure do," Valeria said.

In the morning, everyone jumped out of bed, ready for the beach. But the sun was not shining.

Instead, it was raining. Sixteen people were stuck inside.

"I guess we won't get to feel the soft sand and hot sun," Elena said.

"We won't get to see the big waves, either," said Luisa

"This might be a long day," Tía Carmen said.

"There isn't even a TV here," Luisa said.

"We can still have fun," Sofia said. "Just wait."

She ran upstairs to grab the games. She hurried back down.

"¡Oh dios mío! You only packed games?" Mamá asked. "Where are your clothes?"

"I have one outfit and a swimsuit," Sofia said.

"My sweet Sofia," Abuela said. "You always make things interesting."

"It's okay. We can all share clothes," Camila said. "Right now we need something to play."

"You're right," **Mamá** said. "It looks like Sofia saved the day."

"Let's get playing," Sofia said.

The kids and parents counted paper money. They rolled dice. They moved pieces around game boards. They drew cards.

Everyone was having a great time. They were laughing and yelling and smiling.

"This is so fun!" Sofia said.

They stayed busy until just
after lunch when **Abuela** looked out
the window.

"**¡El sol!**" she said.

"**¡Vámonos!**" **Tío** Miguel shouted.

Ten minutes later, sixteen people were at the beach.

"This is the perfect beach day," **Abuela** said.

"It sure is," Sofia said. "Games, fun, and sun."

CHAPTER 1

The Collection

"¡Atención!" Sofia said. "I need each of you to fill out my question sheet, por favor."

"I can't," Manuel said. "I don't know how to write."

"I'll write for you," Sofia said. "What do you want to be when you grow up?"

"A firefighter," Manuel said.

"Describe yourself in one word," Sofia said.

"Brave!" Manuel said.

Sofia asked more questions. She wrote down Manuel's answers. Then she collected all of the sheets and put them in a cookie tin.

"Why are you putting those papers in a cookie tin?" Manuel asked.

"Because we're making a family time capsule," Sofia said.

"¿Por qué?" Manuel asked.

"So we can have fun in the future by looking at our past," Sofia said.

Sofia's cousins helped her find other things for the time capsule.

"Here's a seashell to remember our beach trips," Alonzo said.

"Here are my favorite drum sticks," Hector said.

"Are you sure?" Sofia asked. "They will stay in the time capsule for ten years."

"Don't worry. I have another pair," Hector said.

"You can take my toy fire truck," Manuel said.

"¡Excelente!" Sofia said.

Except there was a problem. The cookie tin wouldn't close.

"You need something bigger," Alonzo said.

Sofia searched until she found a giant jar of pretzels.

"It's half full," Hector said.

"Sí." Sofia smiled. "Let's start eating!"

CHAPTER 2

Abuela's Addition

Sofia's sisters added **Abuela's arroz con leche** recipe and **Mamá's** piano music to the collection.

Then they helped Sofia decorate the jar.

They used ribbons and paint. They even put some glitter in the bottom of the container.

"**Muy bonito**," Elena said.

Later that day, Sofia's family met in the living room again.

The cousins shared what they had written for the time capsule.

"I wrote about my dream to be an animal doctor," Luisa said. "You know how I love animals."

"I wrote about my dream to be a drummer in a famous band," Hector said as he drummed a beat on the floor.

"I want to be a superhero," Alonzo said running around, pretending to fly.

"And I want to be a TV reporter," Sofia said.

"That is the perfect job for you," **Abuela** said.

"How did you describe

yourselves?" Papá asked.

Alonzo opened his arms.

"Loud!"

Everyone laughed, especially Tía Carmen. She was always complaining about her loud household.

"Curious,'" Sofia answered.

"¡Me gusta!" Abuela said. "That's exactly what my little Sofia is."

Next, Papá held up family pictures. He had some of the house too.

"¡Perfecto!" Sofia said.

Mamá had a bag of dried marigolds. "Because I love my garden," she said.

Abuela raised a handful of colorful envelopes. "I have a letter for each one of my grandchildren."

"Qué bien," Mamá said. "A special message to read in the future."

"About what?" Sofia asked.

"The person you'll be when you're all grown up," Abuela answered.

"Let me see," Sofia begged.

"No peeking!" Abuela winked.

CHAPTER 3

Too Curious

Sofia sealed the time capsule with strong tape and a sign that said, "TOP SECRET!"

The whole family followed her to a closet under the basement stairs.

Papá put the jar on the top shelf. It was the perfect spot for the time capsule. Everyone clapped, except Sofia.

Sofia was busy thinking about **Abuela's** special letters.

"My **abuela** knows everything. She must know the future, too," Sofia thought. "I have to know what she wrote in those letters!"

That night in bed, Sofia could
not sleep.

"Will I be on TV? Will Luisa
be an animal doctor? What about
Hector? How can I wait ten years to
know?" Sofia wondered aloud.

Sofia crept down to the basement in her nightgown. The capsule was way up high. She would have to climb to reach it.

That turned out to be very
noisy. Boxes dropped from lower
shelves.

Mamá and Papá ran downstairs to find a big mess. And under the big mess was Sofia.

"What happened?" Papá asked.

"Lo siento," Sofia said. "I couldn't wait for the future."

"But that's what a time capsule is for," Papá said.

"Yo sé," Sofia said, nodding.

"Why can't you wait?" Mamá asked.

"**Abuela's** letter," Sofia said.

"She knows what I'll be when I

grow up."

"I do too." **Mamá** smiled and

gave Sofia a big hug.

"You do?" Sofia asked.

"Sí," Mamá said. "You'll be curious!"

"Just like you are now," Papá added.

Shopping
~Trip~
Trouble

CHAPTER 1

Backpack Decisions

Sofia hurried to keep up with
her two older sisters, Elena and
Luisa. Elena and Luisa hurried to
keep up with **Mamá**, **Tía** Carmen,
and Sofia's four cousins.

The whole family was going school shopping. They were one big group!

"Stay close," Tía Carmen said. "I don't want anyone to get lost."

They went to the backpack aisle first. The backpacks were hanging from the ceiling to the floor. There were a lot of choices.

"Should I pick one with soccer balls or baseballs?" Hector asked.

"Should I pick zebra stripes or flowers?" Elena asked.

"I pick dinosaurs!" Alonzo said.

"Look at this one!" Manuel yelled. He was pointing to a huge backpack with leopard spots.

"You're in preschool," Hector told his little brother. "That bag is too big for you."

"Maybe you should pick one that is a little smaller," Sofia said.

"Fine," Manuel said, yawning.

Just then Sofia saw a bright green

bag. It had a cool feather design.

"Peacock feathers!" she shouted.

"¡Perfecto!"

"That is perfect," **Mamá** said said. "It has your favorite colors and your favorite animal."

"¡**Vámonos!**" **Tía** Carmen said. "We have more things to buy."

"We sure do!" Sofia said.

CHAPTER 2

Missing Manuel

Sofia was excited to see all the pretty notebooks.

"Mamá," she said. "How many can I have?"

Mamá looked at the school supply list. "Tres."

Three notebooks! That meant
she could have the rainbow, the
silver, and the green!

Mamá read item after item from the list. Everyone was busy picking things out.

Sofia took a break and looked around. Something didn't seem right.

Sofia counted the kids. She came up with three cousins and two sisters. There should be seven kids, not six. She counted the kids again. Oh, no!

"Manuel!" Sofia shouted.
"He's not here!"

"Where is my little Manuel?"
Tía Carmen cried.

"Don't worry," Mamá said.
"We will find him. ¡Vámonos!"

Sofia's family ran around the store. They called Manuel's name.

They rushed around so fast that Hector bumped into Alonzo. Then Alonzo bumped into a shelf of crayons and paint bottles.

Crayons and bottles rolled
everywhere! Sofia, Hector, and
Alonzo tried to clean up, but it
was a big mess.

A store employee came by. "Don't worry. I'll get someone to help," she said.

"**Gracias**," Sofia said.

Sofia's family kept looking for Manuel. They were very worried.

Then they heard a voice over the loudspeaker. That gave Sofia an idea.

"Could we ask the lady on the loudspeaker to help find Manuel?" she asked.

"¡Claro!" Tía Carmen said.

"Follow me!"

CHAPTER 3

Back to the Backpacks

"Attention! A four-year-old boy is missing. He has black hair and is wearing a blue shirt. Please come to the front of the store if you've seen him."

After the announcement, an older man came up to them.

"I saw a little boy in the backpack aisle," he said. "He had black hair and a blue shirt."

"¡Gracias!" Mamá said. "¡Vámonos!"

When the family reached the backpack aisle, they only saw the huge wall of backpacks.

No Manuel.

Baby Mariela began to cry.
Tía Carmen brushed Mariela's
cheek. "I know. It's your nap
time," she said.

As Tía Carmen comforted the
baby, Sofia thought of something.

"It's Manuel's nap time, too," she said.

That's when she saw a row of backpacks on the bottom move. Sofia pushed one aside. Manuel was underneath, fast asleep.

Tía Carmen grabbed Manuel.

"You scared me!"

Everyone gathered around

Manuel to hug him. He rubbed his

eyes. "I want to go home," he said.

When the family got back home, they had lunch together. Just as they finished, Sofia asked, "What about our school supplies?"

Mamá slapped her forehead.

"We left everything in the shopping

cart at the store!" she said.

"Can we go back?" Sofia asked.

"Mañana," Tía Carmen said. "I'm too tired now."

"Sí," Mamá agreed. "Tomorrow."

"What if the things we picked are gone?" Sofia asked.

"Por favor," Elena said. "My butterfly notebooks were so pretty."

"I want the shark pencil case," Hector said.

"And I really love that backpack with the feathers on it," Sofia said.

Everyone remembered how long it took to choose school supplies.

Mamá picked up her purse.
"¡Vámonos!"

Sofia and Manuel were the
first ones out the door.

Spanish Glossary

abuela — grandmother

arroz con leche — rice pudding

atención — attention

claro — of course

el sol — the sun

excelente — great

gracias — thank you

lo siento — I'm sorry

mamá — mom

mañana — tomorrow

me gusta — I like it

muy bonito — very pretty

no más — no more

oh dios mío — oh my goodness

papá — dad

perfecto — perfect

por favor — please

por qué — why

qué bien — how nice

sí — yes

silencio — silence

tía — aunt

tío — uncle

tres — three

vámonos — let's go

yo sé — I know

About the Author

Jacqueline Jules is the award-winning author of thirty children's books, including *No English* (2012 Forward National Literature Award), *Zapato Power: Freddie Ramos Takes Off* (2010 CYBILS Literary Award, Maryland Blue Crab Young Reader Honor Award, and ALSC Great Early Elementary Reads), and *Freddie Ramos Makes a Splash* (named on 2013 List of Best Children's Books of the Year by Bank Street College Committee).

When not reading, writing, or teaching, Jacqueline enjoys time with her family in Northern Virginia.

About the Illustrator

Kim Smith has worked in magazines, advertising, animation, and children's gaming. She studied illustration at the Alberta College of Art and Design in Calgary, Alberta.

Kim is the illustrator of the upcoming middle-grade mystery series *The Ghost and Max Monroe,* the picture book *Over the River and Through the Woods*, and the cover of the forthcoming middle-grade novel *How to Make a Million*. She resides in Calgary, Alberta.

See you soon!

¡Nos vemos pronto!